Bea Breaks Barriers!

How Florence Beatrice Price's
Music Triumphed
Over Prejudice

Caitlin DeLems

Illustrated by Tonya Engel

CALKINS CREEK
AN IMPRINT OF ASTRA BOOKS FOR YOUNG READERS
New York

NOTE
Florence B. Price uses the words Colored and Negro, common terms for her times, in her writings. These words were also included on signs in the South to segregate the races.

*I have an unwavering and compelling faith
that a national music very beautiful and very American
can come from the melting pot
just as the nation itself has done.*

—Florence B. Price

Florence Beatrice Smith was not like other girls in Little Rock, Arkansas. She sat at the keyboard. Tapped her feet. Drummed her fingers. And played tune after tune. Sunup till sundown, sounds delighted Bea.

Steamboats paddle. Mournful whistles.
Whip-poor-wills warble. Katydids chorus.
Juba dance and jammin' banjo rhythms.
She turned them all into music.

Mother dabbled in singing, taught little Bea piano.
Sold property and proudly owned a café. Father was
a published author, a teacher, and the inventor of
a peach pitter. But above all, he was Little Rock's
most popular dentist.

Father could barely squeeze all his patients inside his office.

Bea could barely squeeze all the music she craved inside her head. Negro spirituals. Classical music. Folk songs. Even the foot-stomping and clapping sounds of Pattin' Juba.

Most hotels in the South turned away Black people, so Bea's father hosted overnight guests—big-name orators, artists, and musicians.

When ragtime performer John William "Blind" Boone came to stay, Bea raced to the keyboard. Together they jammed. Boone tickled the ivories with his ragged rhythms, and Bea pounded out her little tunes.

And once when "Blind" Boone bid goodbye, he tucked Bea's newly composed ditty inside his pocket.

At her first official recital, four-year-old Bea brought down the house—*her* house. Black girls did not give recitals in public buildings or hardly ever attend lessons at music studios. Not in Arkansas.

In the South, signs shouted COLORED ONLY and WHITES ONLY.

Separate seating areas—on buses and trains. In libraries, theaters, and diners.

Separate playing areas—at parks and pools. Separate everything—even public schools.

When Bea attended an all-Black public school for children six to sixteen, she soaked up every assignment. Limited textbooks and supplies—and no library!—did not hold back Bea. She sailed to the top of her class.

Bea earned her high school diploma a year early and took home the valedictorian award. She realized there was "no opportunity open" in the South, so she set her sights northward. Set her sights on being a composer.

Barely sixteen, Bea boarded a train to Boston and the New England Conservatory of Music—the crème de la crème of music schools.

When she arrived, she found herself among
two thousand students.
Two were Black.

Bea remembered the soothing organ music back home in Little Rock. She started as a concert organ major. Added piano and headed for a double major! Published a composition. ALL in her first year.

HISTORY

frican Music

Musicale!

PHON

MUSICOLOG

Nothing would keep Bea from music, from doing her best.

Bea crammed in music theory and harmony. Enrolled in composition courses and studied the great composers.

Dug deep into her roots.

Put in a little rhythm.

Added a little spiritual.

And spun a classical music style all her own.

Negro folk songs fused with southern accents "flavored" Bea's music. Her organ performances brought audiences to their feet.

Bea graduated with honors in three years and was the only student in the class of 1906 to earn TWO degrees—one in organ, the other in piano.

Some alums set off to marry. Others remained in the big city to chase their careers.

But for Bea, it was high time for change . . .

Cool, calm, calculated, Bea headed back to Little Rock and her musical roots—determined to help her community. She taught in several Black colleges. Directed a music department at a university. Brought notable artists to campuses.

And when young lawyer Thomas Jewell Price swept Bea off her feet, she left college behind. Married him, raised two daughters, and kept right on composing.

In the 1920s, most of Bea's classical compositions remained atop her piano. Countless publishers had cast them aside.

Bea struggled. And so did the country.

Hard times surged across America and battered Bea's hometown. There were few jobs and little money—and, worst of all, violence aimed at Little Rock's Black citizens.

Bea packed up her family—as did many! Fled north to safety—and a fresh start.

Chicago! Alive with a BOOMING community of Black artists and musicians, AND Marian Anderson—the world-famous contralto who visited the city often.

Bea and Marian connected like melody and harmony. Bea wrote music to celebrate her African heritage. Marian sent Bea's songs soaring.

Bea focused on her career more than ever. To scrape together earnings, she composed commercial jingles. Taught piano—even violin. Played organ for silent films and arranged music for radio orchestras. And still had time to create her first symphony!

Bea entered the symphony in a major music competition and won first place! Her prize captured the attention of Frederick Stock, conductor of the Chicago Symphony Orchestra.

In early summer of 1933, Bea sat in a packed house at the Chicago's World Fair. Maestro Stock's baton swung into action. The orchestra's melody of horns rose and fell. And silky violins set the mood. Blended folk, spiritual, and Juba dance rhythms swept through Bea's Symphony in E Minor.

After the final note "the large audience filled to the brim with music lovers of all races, rang out in applause."

Outstanding composer . . . discovered! —The Winnetka Talk

[First] Race woman . . . to have an orchestral work performed by a major American orchestra. —Chicago Defender

A faultless work . . . worthy of a place in the repertory. —Chicago Daily News

The Chicago orchestra performance set Bea's music in motion. Publishers and conductors marveled. Spectators lent an ear.

But over the next six years, Bea's popularity shot up and down like scales on a piano.

She pulled out a fresh music sheet. Composed
a new version of the Negro spiritual "My Soul's
Been Anchored in de Lord." And sent the
arrangement to friend Marian Anderson.

Little did Bea know her life was about to change . . .

On April 9, 1939, Marian Anderson, "denied the use of Constitution Hall because of her race," sang to the nation from the steps of the Lincoln Memorial. Marian chose Bea's spiritual as the ROUSING grand finale.

Florence B. Price's song "rang out" to over seventy-five thousand people. Poured out over radio waves to even more. MILLIONS heard Bea's music that blustery Easter Sunday!

My soul's been anchored in de Lord;
Until I've reached the mountain top,
My soul's been anchored in de Lord.

AUTHOR'S NOTE

Florence B. Price's arrangement of the spiritual "My Soul's Been Anchored in de Lord" propelled her into the national limelight following Marian Anderson's 1939 Easter Sunday performance. Anderson sang Price's sensation over one hundred times onstage worldwide, often as the closing piece.

From late 1927 to the mid-1940s, Price's name appeared regularly in the most influential national Black newspaper in America, the *Chicago Defender*. The *Defender* referred to her as the "Dean of Negro Women Composers of the Middle West." Although her music was in the spotlight, personal times were turbulent for Bea.

Career-driven, single, and in dire financial straits, Price moved from place to place in Chicago with two young daughters in tow. More than once, her network of artist friends opened their doors to her. Later, Bea and her children moved to a small apartment on the seventh floor of the Abraham Lincoln Center, a low-to-moderate-income community house where other trailblazing artists lived. As the center's expert music teacher, Bea had a large studio on the sixth floor. At times her students numbered close to one hundred.

During the Great Depression and World War II, Black composers found it more difficult to have their large-scale works published or performed. Resilient, Bea produced a flurry of small-scale works for a variety of settings and taught music lessons to get by. She also published instructional piano pieces and composed two symphonies and a piano concerto. Bea persisted. She always sought ways to improve her craft.

Bea joined the National Association of Negro Musicians (NANM) and battled injustice and inequality for years. She broke racial barriers by integrating several all-white musical organizations. Memberships brought more recognition to her music. Ensembles, esteemed artists, and professional friends performed even her unpublished works. She wanted her music heard.

Florence B. Price's reputation as the most well-known Black woman composer broadened—yet one lifelong goal eluded her. The old-guard East Coast establishments—the Boston Symphony Orchestra, New York Philharmonic, and Philadelphia Orchestra—had not performed her large-scale works. To have one of these orchestras play her music would validate her entire career as an artist.

On November 6, 1943, Bea wrote her fourth letter to Maestro Serge Koussevitzky of the Boston Symphony Orchestra urging him to perform her music.

My dear Dr. Koussevitzky:

Unfortunately the work of a woman composer is preconceived by many to be light, frothy, lacking in depth, logic and virility. Add to that the incident of race—I have Colored blood in my veins—and you will understand some of the difficulties that confront one in such a position. . . .

I ask no concessions because of race or sex, and am willing to abide by a decision based solely on [the] worth of my work.

Will you be kind enough to examine a score of mine?

Very truly yours,
(Mrs.) Florence B. Price

She sent her music scores to Koussevitzky, "hoping mightily" he'd approve, but the eminent conductor's orchestra never performed her music. By the late 1940s, Bea's name appeared less often in the *Defender*. Still, she continued to network among artists and compose. Burdened by poor health she finished several last works, including Violin Concerto No. 2.

Price's ever-popular spiritual arrangement for solo voice and orchestra was made instantly famous by Marian Anderson.

MY SOUL'S BEEN ANCHORED
in de Lord.

Negro Spiritual
Arr. by Florence B. Price

Carl Fischer. Inc. New York.
No. 22—24 lines.

In 1953, Bea planned a European trip to accept a music award. On May 24, only days prior to her departure, she entered Chicago's St. Luke's Hospital where she died of heart failure on June 3. Two days later, a "simple and brief" service was held at her church, Grace Presbyterian, followed by burial in an unmarked plot at Chicago's Lincoln Cemetery.

Florence B. Price's music crossed every genre except opera. She composed around three hundred works for solo piano, organ, voice, orchestra, chorus, and chamber ensembles, including arrangements of spirituals. Her music style pleased audiences with its blend of classical music, Negro spirituals and African American rhythms—especially dance.

After her death, Bea's name faded from the mainstream music world and most of her work disappeared—lost for well over half a century, until . . .

In 2009, a couple purchased an abandoned bungalow sixty miles south of Chicago. Looters had ransacked it, leaving behind a trove of dozens and dozens of musical scores curled and yellowed from age. Each score carried the same signature—*Florence Beatrice Price*.

Well-deserved recognition of Price's accomplishments is on the rise. The *Caged Bird: The Life and Music of Florence B. Price*, an Emmy-nominated documentary produced by James Greeson, DMA, was released in 2015.

In March 2019, the Boston Symphony Orchestra performed three movements from Florence B. Price's Symphony No. 3—*eighty-four* years after Maestro Koussevitzky had received her request.

One year later, in August 2020, the inaugural International Florence Price Festival (Price Fest), dedicated to preserving Bea's legacy and music opened online to keep the celebration of her music alive. And it was only the beginning.

In 2022, the Philadelphia Orchestra won their first Best Orchestral Performance Grammy for their Florence Price album. A year later, the New York Youth Orchestra won in the same category for their album of works by Black women composers, including two of Price's compositions.

For almost a century, Black musicians have not forgotten Florence Price. Today, music lovers everywhere can appreciate her phenomenal works.

The remarkable crescendo of public interest in Florence B. Price's music is proof she triumphed in her lifelong fight for equality as a Black female composer.

This photograph of Bea was taken around 1940.

MUSIC GLOSSARY

arrangement: Adapting or changing a song to put a new, unique twist on it.

**art song: A vocal music composition, usually written for one singer accompanied by piano; most often a poem or text set to music in the classical tradition.

**chamber music: Music written to be performed by a small group of three or four musicians and usually played in a small room.

classical music (also known as art music): A style of serious music rooted in the European tradition starting around 1750; different from jazz, pop, or folk music.

*concerto: A composition for a soloist accompanied by an orchestra.

contralto: The lowest singing voice of a female.

*crescendo: A slow, steady increase in the loudness of music.

ditty: A simple, short song or tune.

folk song: Traditional music/songs common to a people, region, or country passed down orally from one generation to the next.

harmony: Notes sounded at the same time; often in support of a melody.

jingle: Catchy repetition of musical sounds used to help promote a product on commercials.

Florence B. Smith graduated from the New England Conservatory of Music in three years, instead of four, and was the only student to receive two diplomas. Bea is in the second row, the third person from the right.

Juba also known as Pattin' Juba or hambone: An African dance (*Giouba*) common among the Southern plantation slaves consisting of rhythmic hand clapping, slapping/patting of thighs and body, and foot stomping; often accompanied by folk melodies, rhymes, and songs.

melody: A series of musically satisfying single notes, played one after another to make a tune.

music theory: The study of how to compose music.

Negro spirituals: A genre of religious folk songs evolving from the enslavement of African people in the American South during the late eighteenth and nineteenth century.

orchestra: A large group of instrumentalists with stringed, woodwind, brass, and percussion instruments.

radio orchestra: An orchestra hired to play music on the radio for various programming.

radio waves: Electromagnetic waves that travel through space. Radio waves help transmit music to radios and television, as well as communicate with air-traffic controllers and astronauts.

ragtime: Music that uses a special kind of rhythm called syncopation; syncopated rhythm sounds as though the music suddenly stops and starts; popular from 1895 until 1918.

*score (music score)**:** A copy of music a conductor uses with parts for all instruments.

symphony: A large-scale composition performed by an orchestra; usually in four movements. Also, another name for an orchestra.

tickle the ivories: Play the piano; refers to the white piano keys, traditionally made of ivory.

Little is known about this photograph, but it is believed to have been taken around 1906, the year nineteen-year-old Bea graduated from New England Conservatory.

TIMELINE

1887 April 9—Florence Beatrice Smith (Price) born in Little Rock, Arkansas. Bea lives with parents, Dr. James H. Smith and Florence Irene Gulliver Smith, and ten-year-old brother, Charles W. H. Smith.

1890 Three-year-old Bea's first piano lesson given by Mother.

Over the years, Bea often entertains Father's notable guests at the piano.

1891 First formal recital performance at age four given at her home in Little Rock.

Date Unknown—It is believed Bea first attends St. Mary's Convent and School in Little Rock.

About 1897—At fifth grade, transfers to Union School, an all-Black public school in Little Rock.

Florence Beatrice Smith with her mother, Florence Irene Gulliver Smith. This is believed to be one of the earliest known photographs of Bea.

1897 Bea attends after-hours music lessons, likely including organ, at St. Mary's Convent. At ten, plays art songs and composes music. Instruction centers on classical music, later expands to include multiple music styles.

1902 Graduates as valedictorian from Capitol Hill School in Little Rock.

1903 September—Begins New England Conservatory of Music (NEC) in Boston, Massachusetts. Enrolls in composition courses and receives payment for music piece.

NEC director George W. Chadwick awards Bea a private scholarship to study music composition with him.

1904 Over the next two years, Bea is often selected to represent her class at the New England Conservatory recitals; performs both at the piano and organ.

1906 June 20—Graduates from New England Conservatory of Music with two degrees.

Moves home to Little Rock. From 1906 to 1910 teaches nearby at several Black colleges.

1910 Head of the Music Department at Clark University in Atlanta, Georgia, for two years.

1912 Returns to Little Rock; September 9, marries attorney Thomas Jewell Price; teaches piano from her home studio and composes short pieces.

1917 Firstborn Thomas Jr. dies in infancy. Daughters Florence Louise born in 1917 and Edith in 1921.

About 1918—Arkansas Music Teachers Association denies Bea membership due to her race.

1920 *Active member of the National Association of Negro Musicians.

This portrait of Florence Beatrice Smith was possibly taken in 1902—the year of her high school graduation.

1924 President/director of the Little Rock Club of Musicians serving the Black community.

1926 Piano piece "In the Land of Cotton" ties for second place in *Opportunity* magazine's Holstein Prize contest.

1927 Between late 1927 and early 1928, Bea moves to Chicago with her children; Thomas Price follows later.

First Black woman to integrate the Illinois Federation of Music Clubs, the Chicago Club of Women Organists, and the Musicians Club of Women.

1928 G. Schirmer, a major firm, publishes Price's piano piece "At the Cotton Gin."

1929 Great Depression begins. Wins scholarship to study orchestration at Chicago's American Conservatory of Music.

1931 Divorces, remains in Chicago with her two young daughters.

1932 Wins first prize in two categories of the Rodman Wanamaker competition: $500 for Symphony in E Minor and $250 for Piano Sonata in E Minor.

1933 June 15—Chicago Symphony Orchestra premieres Price's Symphony in E Minor, under conductor Frederick Stock at the Century of Progress Exposition (Chicago World's Fair).

1939 April 9—Marian Anderson sings Price's arrangement of "My Soul's Been Anchored in the Lord" at the Lincoln Memorial in Washington, DC.

Late 1940s–early 1950s—U.S. Marine Band regularly performs Price's "Three Negro Dances."

1953 June 3—At sixty-six, Florence B. Price dies at St. Luke's Hospital in Chicago.

National Association of Negro Musicians continues to present Price's music after her death.

1964 The building of the Florence B. Price Elementary School in Chicago honors Price's legacy as a Black woman composer and Chicago musician; unveiling ceremony includes selections from her Piano Concerto No. 1, Violin Concerto No. 2, and a children's song, "It's Snowing."

About 2000—The Women's Philharmonic directed by Apo Hsu makes landmark recording of Price's orchestral music.

2009 Price's missing orchestral scores, vocal and piano music, and all chamber music discovered.

University of Arkansas Special Collections Library in Fayetteville acquires Price's lost music. They sort and repair the water-damaged scores and make them available to musicians and researchers.

2018 Price is inducted into the Arkansas Women's Hall of Fame; the Arkansas State Music Teachers Association, which had earlier denied Price membership, honors her.

Music publisher G. Schirmer, Inc., acquires rights to Price catalog.

2022 Music Director Yannick Nézet-Séguin and the Philadelphia Orchestra's recording of Florence Price's Symphony Nos. 1 and 3 is awarded a Grammy.

2023 Music Director Michael Repper and the New York Youth Symphony's recording, including two of Price's works, wins a Grammy.

Present Day—Distinguished orchestras, as well as youth and community groups, continuously perform Price's music.

*Florence B. Price was an active member in other music organizations during her lifetime as well, including two chapters of NANM: Chicago Music Association and R. Nathaniel Dett Club; American Society of Composers, Authors, and Publishers (ASCAP); National Association for American Composers and Conductors; and American Composers' Alliance.

In 1910, after the death of her father, twenty-three-year-old Florence B. Smith left Little Rock and accepted a prestigious position as head of the Music Department at Clark University in Atlanta. She is seated in the second row, the first chair on left.

ARTISTS WHO MADE UP BEA'S WORLD

Marian Anderson (1897–1993) (below): World-renowned African American classical vocalist who mainly performed spirituals. Price sent Anderson more than fifty of her songs, many of which she premiered.

Estella Bonds (n.d.): President of Chicago Music Association in late 1930s; organist and pianist. Black artists, writers, and musicians often gathered at her large home. Bonds welcomed Price and her daughters to stay during desperate financial times and supported her career.

Margaret Bonds (1913–1972): Noted American composer, pianist, teacher. Studied piano and composition with Price; they often performed together. Best known for her spirituals for solo voice. Daughter of Estella Bonds.

John William "Blind" Boone (1864–1927): Born in Missouri to an enslaved mother. A blind African American pianist and composer of many published works. Played 8,400 concerts.

George Whitefield Chadwick (1854–1931): Eminent American composer/musician, conductor, and New England Conservatory director. He saw Bea as a promising composer.

Samuel Coleridge-Taylor (1875–1912): English-born composer, conductor, and professor of music. Taylor's British and African heritage influenced his compositions and inspired Price.

Frederick Douglass (about 1818–1895): Born enslaved in Maryland. Noted author, orator, and a leader in the abolitionist movement. Famous intellectual of his time. Guest at young Bea's home.

W. E. B. Du Bois (1868–1963): American civil rights activist and writer. Like Bea, Du Bois believed that Negro spirituals were the sole American music. Du Bois and Bea corresponded.

Antonín Dvořák (1841–1904): One of the greatest Czech composers of the nineteenth century. Artistic director and professor of music at the National Conservatory of Music in New York from 1892–1895. His music strongly influenced Bea.

Maude Roberts George (n.d.): *Chicago Defender* music critic and 1932 president of the Chicago Music Association. George's regular reviews of Price helped to elevate her career.

Serge Koussevitzky (1874–1951): Russian-born composer and conductor of the Boston Symphony Orchestra for twenty-five years (1924–1949). Price made multiple requests to have Koussevitzky review her scores and perform her music.

Charlotte (Lottie) Andrews Stephens (1854–1951): Born enslaved in Arkansas. First Black teacher in Little Rock; taught for seventy years. Bea flourished under Stephens's instruction.

William Grant Still (1895–1978): American composer and arranger. First American Black man to have a symphony performed by a major orchestra. Bea's lifelong friend.

Frederick Stock (1872–1942): German-born composer. Notable American conductor of the Chicago Symphony Orchestra from 1905 to 1942. Significant in advancing Price's career.

ACKNOWLEDGMENTS

Sincere appreciation to expert Douglas Shadle, PhD, Vanderbilt University Blair School of Music for his essential contributions to the creation of Bea's story: expertise, abundant patience, and generous time and thoughtful responses to numerous inquiries and multiple manuscript reviews.

With gratitude to James R. Greeson, DMA, University of Arkansas (UARK), Fayetteville, for his considerate time, patience, reviews, and endless assistance in providing a wealth of documentation for my story to unfold; Alexandra Kori Hill, PhD, musicology, University of North Carolina at Chapel Hill, for keen insight, dedication, and meticulous review to ensure a finer account; Liane Curtis, PhD, musicology, for her passionate introduction to Price.

In gratitude to Barbara Garvey Jackson, PhD, musicology, UARK, Fayetteville; Linda Holzer, DMus, UARK, Little Rock; Lori Birrell (former head), Geoffery Starks (former research coordinator), and Casiday Long, research services coordinator, Special Collections, Mullins Library, UARK, Fayetteville; Betsy Johnson, MA, CA, collections management archivist, and Maureen Skorupa Keyes, Institute Community Archivist, Sisters of Mercy of the Americas Archives, Little Rock; and Sr. Joan Pfauser, RSM, Mount St. Mary Academy, Little Rock, for aid in my research.

Special thanks to Highlights Foundation's Kent and George Brown, and Jo Lloyd for creating a magical environment for my story to unfold; Carolyn Yoder's fellow writers/retreaters for camaraderie; Kathryn M. Yoder, unforgettable pillar of knowledge, passion; Jeri Ferris and Kathy Cannon Wiechman, for comments on a work in progress and steadfast support.

With deepest regard to my Calkins Creek editor, Carolyn P. Yoder, for pearls of wisdom, skillful guidance, and steady patience throughout multiple revisions; to Barbara Grzeslo, art director, for her remarkable gift of design; and to Kerry McManus for her expertise.

Fond appreciation to my mother, Irene, for her love of words, kindred spirit, and enthusiasm along the way; and with heartfelt gratitude to Ryan, Eva, and Laura.

Tender gratefulness to my husband, Tom, for his unflinching patience, support, and feedback, laughter and ease.

—CD

ILLUSTRATOR'S NOTE

It was an immense delight for me to have the opportunity to research and illustrate the brilliant and inspirational life of Florence Beatrice Price! While capturing the sense of how life might have felt, sounded, or appeared to a young gifted Black girl who was growing up in the deeply segregated south, I wished to give the reader a sense of Florence's disappointments and challenges as well as her triumphs and victories.

I tried to be precise about the times and era. What type of clothing was worn? What type of piano would an average family have owned? Fashion was transitioning from the stiff Victorian Age into a time of more freedoms and liberties for women. While women were finally beginning to be introduced to areas of society previously only occupied by men, like sports and music, Black people were never fully able to forget their limited freedoms. Despite these limitations, Florence shined! While addressing these details, I thought that adding a touch of Art Nouveau and Art Deco, the styles of art that would have adorned the walls during Florence's lifetime and career, would artistically bring it all together.

—TE

SELECTED BIBLIOGRAPHY*

All quotations used in the book can be found in the following sources marked with two asterisks (**).

Books and Papers

Ammer, Christine. *Unsung: A History of Women in American Music*, 2nd ed. Portland, OR: Amadeus Press, 2001.

**Brown, Rae Linda. *The Heart of a Woman: The Life and Music of Florence B. Price.* Urbana: University of Illinois Press, 2020.

**Interview with Dr. Rae Linda Brown on the "Life and Music of Florence Price," by James R. Gleason in Fayetteville, AR, June 4, 2014.

Jackson, Barbara Garvey. "Florence Price, Composer." *The Black Perspective in Music*, Spring 1977, 30–43.

Pendle, Karin, ed. *Women & Music: A History*, 2nd ed. Bloomington: Indiana University Press, 2001.

Shadle, Douglas. "Plus Ça Change: Florence B. Price in the #BlackLivesMatter Era." *New Music Box*, New Music USA, February 20, 2019. nmbx.newmusicusa.org/plus-ca-change-florence-b-price-in-the-blacklivesmatter-era.

Articles/Newspapers

Bartlette, DeLani. "Who was Florence Price?" Interview with Er-Gene Kahng, professor of violin, January 12, 2018, University of Arkansas, Arkansas Research. https://web.archive.org/web/20201030235857/https://arkansasresearch.uark.edu/who-was-florence-price.

Brascher, Nahum Daniel. "Roland Hayes Concert Shows Progress of Race in Music." *Chicago Defender*, June 24, 1933.

Brown, Rae Linda, and Wayne D. Shirley, eds. "Florence Price 1887–1953, Symphonies Nos. 1 and 3." Middleton, WI: A–R Editions, 2008.

Dykema, Dan. "Florence Beatrice Smith Price (1887–1953)." *CALS Encyclopedia of Arkansas*, Central Arkansas Library System, September 10, 2018. encyclopediaofarkansas.net/entries/florence-beatrice-smith-price-1742.

"Florence Beatrice Price: A Closer Look with Musicologist Douglas Shadle." Naxos of America Inc., January 9, 2019. naxosusa.com/florence-beatrice-price-a-closer-look-with-musicologist-douglas-shadle.

Holzer, Linda. "This is what diversity sounds like." *Piano Magazine* (formerly *Clavier Companion*), November 2018. claviercompanion.com/article-details/this-is-what-diversity-sounds-like.

Ross, Alex. "The Rediscovery of Florence Price: How an African-American Composer's Work Was Saved from Destruction." *The New Yorker*, January 29, 2018. newyorker.com/magazine/2018/02/05/the-rediscovery-of-florence-price.

Walwyn, Dr. Karen. "Biography of Florence Beatrice Price: A Fight for Recognition." florenceprice.com/biography.

Archival Sources: Materials and Letter Collections

**University of Arkansas, Fayetteville, Mullins Library Special Collections, Florence Beatrice Smith Price Materials. Gift of Price's daughter, Florence Price Robinson, and collected by Mary Dengler Hudgins and Barbara Garvey Jackson. Papers include correspondence of Price and Florence Price Robinson; letters; diary fragments; news clippings; music programs; music scores; and photographs. Materials are housed in sets: MC988, 988a, and 988b.

**Florence B. Price to Dr. H. Clay Chenault, dean of the University of Arkansas School of Medicine. Letter of August 25, 1948. University of Arkansas for Medical Sciences, Little Rock. Edith Irby Jones Alumni File Collection.

Video

Greeson, James R. DMA, director and producer. *The Caged Bird: The Life and Music of Florence B. Price.* 2015 (DVD).

Websites to Visit

Classics for Kids. Use the drop-down menu from the Home Page for a variety of interactive links. Listen to the music of great composers and musicians, the instruments of the orchestra, and compose your own music. classicsforkids.com; classicsforkids.com/composers_letter/?initial=P.

Music Historians and Experts Interviewed/Consulted

Liane Curtis, PhD, musicology. President, Women's Philharmonic Advocacy.

James R. Greeson, DMA. Professor Emeritus of Music, University of Arkansas, Fayetteville.

Alexandra Kori Hill, PhD, musicology. Music Historian, Diversity Reader, University of North Carolina at Chapel Hill.

Douglas Shadle, PhD, Associate Professor of Musicology, Chair, Department of Musicology and Ethnomusicology, Vanderbilt University Blair School of Music.

*Websites active at time of publication

PICTURE CREDITS

To Ruth and Ginger—forever grateful
And for a world vision of unwavering equality —*CD*

Dedicated to every dreamer who dared to imagine that dream into existence —*TE*

For information about permission to reproduce selections from this book,
please contact permissions@astrapublishinghouse.com.

Calkins Creek
An imprint of Astra Books for Young Readers,
a division of Astra Publishing House
astrapublishinghouse.com
Printed in China

ISBN: 978-1-63592-427-5 (hc)
ISBN: 978-1-6626-8065-6 (eBook)
Library of Congress Control Number: 2023914434

First edition
10 9 8 7 6 5 4 3 2 1

Design by Barbara Grzeslo
The text is set in ITC Avant Garde Gothic.
The illustrations are done in acrylic and oil (mixed media) on paper.